For Deek – L.G.

EGMONT

We bring stories to life

First published in Great Britain 2018 by Egmont UK Limited,
The Yellow Building, 1 Nicholas Road,
London W11 4AN
www.egmont.co.uk

Text copyright © Louise Greig 2018
Illustrations copyright © Ashling Lindsay 2018
The Author and Illustrator hereby assert their moral rights.

ISBN 9781 4052 8659 6 (Paperback)

Between Tick and Tock

LOUISE GREIG

ASHLING LINDSAY

EGMONT

Tick-tock, tick-tock.
The city shouts, *Hurry!*
Can't stop! No time!

LIBRARY

Trams grumble, trains growl,
Out of the way!

The streets see only Grey.

Lonely twirls in a park.

Lost rolls under a bench.

Stray whimpers faintly.

Stuck miaows from a tree.

The city is too busy to see.

But, high above the bustle,
where weary wings take rest,
are eyes that watch.

And hands that know — it's time to pause the clock.

And for one tiny moment,
between tick and tock . . .

The city shudders to a STOP.

Hushhhhh swells like a silent sea,
swallowing every sound.

Eyes close.

Everyone, everything,
snaps to a standstill.

But Liesel moves.

She weaves where Frenzy is now Freeze.
Down steep stone steps to the street below.

No one sees.
No one knows how a garden grows in a blink.

Green, Pink
and Purple glow
as Grey slinks away.

The little alleyway feels pretty
and whispers, *Thank you.*

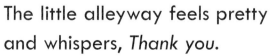

While the clock holds its breath,
Liesel threads through the stillness.

Two ladies in hats stand like statues.
Don't argue. There's plenty for each of you,
and crumbs for a speck of sparrow too.

And, Up comes Down
as Liesel's three gentle
words carry Stuck
back to the ground . . .

Next, Down goes Up —
*Oh, baby blackbird,
you have jumped
from your nest too
soon. Wait for your
feathers to grow and
your wings to beat strong.*

All safe now.

But, the silent city still wears a frown.
A smile is flipped upside down by Worry.

CITY
LIBRARY

It's alright, murmurs Liesel,
The Book of Tigers
is back on time.

The librarian loves this book too! When the
clock starts again the city will ROAR, but you
can talk tigers together – in whispers.

Outside, Liesel dashes and darts to match and mend.

WHIRL! Lonely finds a friend.

PLINK! Who will find this lucky penny?

There! Now a worried duck has her dear ducklings back.

Sometimes a city needs a hand.

Two tiny arms reach out to Lost.

And sometimes a city needs a little nudge.

Oh, cries Liesel. *A kite should be soaring. Up,* up, up!

As for a precious purple passenger . . .
Please, driver, whispers Liesel,
Stop by a lilac bush.

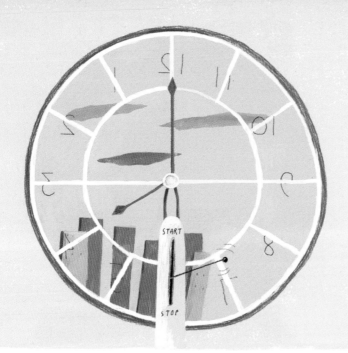

But, the clock is calling Liesel back,
for a city cannot stay at Stop,
stuck between tick and tock.

Clutching a bundle with two velvet ears,

Liesel races home.

And from her window high above,
she blows Grey far away.

As tick turns to tock, suddenly,
silence splutters back to sound,
eyes open, stillness stirs and stumbles,
and the city rumbles back to life.

Tick-tock, tick-tock.
The city sings and sparkles.

An alleyway hears –
Oh, how pretty!

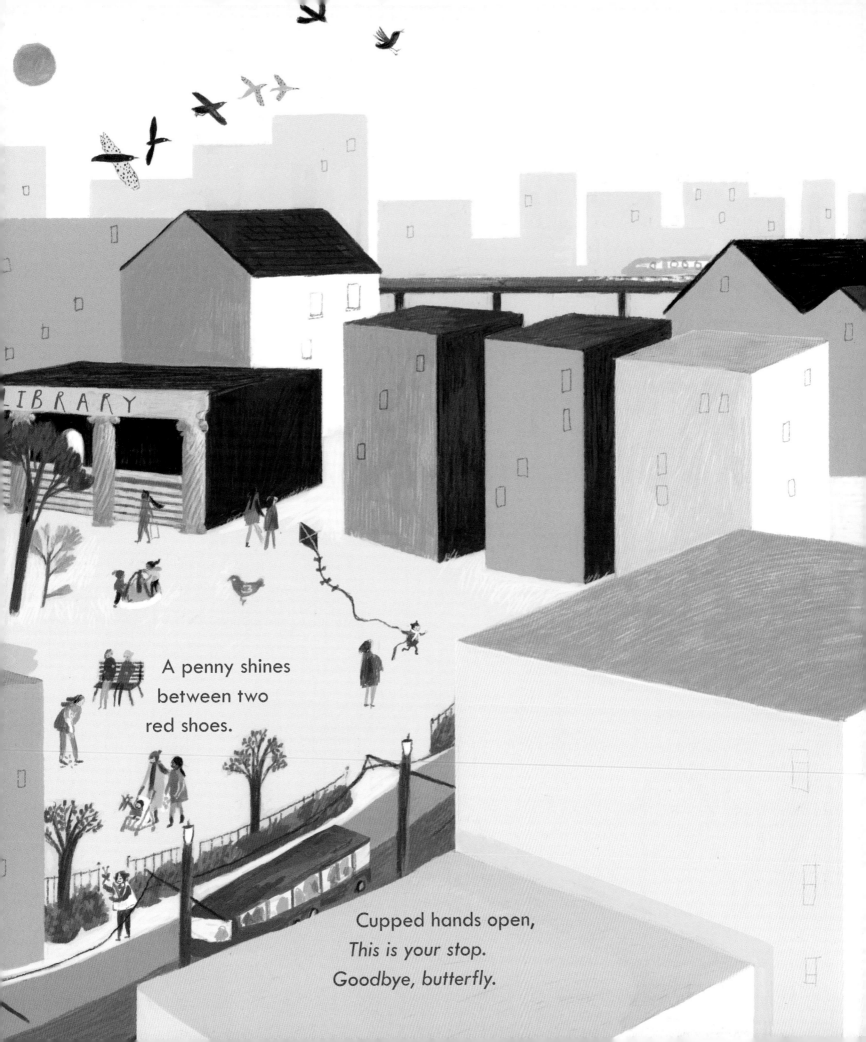

LIBRARY

A penny shines
between two
red shoes.

Cupped hands open,
This is your stop.
Goodbye, butterfly.

Up, up high above the bustle,
where wide wings soar,
Stray learns his name, even
smaller than him – *Ben*.

And if the streets should lose
their way again, kind hands
know what to do. Liesel will
just reach up . . .

Tick-tock, tick-tock. Tick—

Who says a city never stops?